In His Presence

Tonya Alston

I dedicate this book to my monthly faithful callers that have spent time over the year, growing in their faith. Throughout the year, they participated in the teachings, learning about who they are, and strengthening their relationship with God. They gained a deeper understanding of God through his words. I pray that this devotional will change the life of every reader. I pray that hearts will be opened to receive the words that are written in this book. Be Free. Love Deep and Know that God is Present with you.

INTRODUCTION

Most people want to know if God is near, does he know my every move, and is he guiding my life. Knowing what God's plan for our lives is a frequent desire when you are seeking to know your purpose and direction. God, what are the plans for my life? As the end of 2018 approached, I had similar questions. I needed God to direct my path; I needed answers about the direction of my life. So, I started to seek him in a significant way. Praying and reading my Bible was standard, but now I needed a more profound sense of knowing and hearing from God. Hearing from God meant that I needed to build a stronger relationship with him if I want to truly be in his presence. If I was going to hear from God during this time of need, I needed to re-evaluate my relationship with him. Do I really know God, I asked? What does it mean to be in his presence? These questions were essential to an old church girl like me. I needed to know! This book will teach and guide you on how to get closer to God by getting into his presence while learning the foundations of hearing from him.

CHAPTER 1

The Presence of God

The presence of God started from the beginning when God made man and woman in his image and likeness. God created us for his pleasure, for us to know him and worship him, so it pleased God to create. Getting to know God is simple; it is not some magical conjure. It is through fellowship with him by worshipping, praying, reading the Word of God, and meditating. When you fellowship with God, you are spending time with him building a relationship. God already knows us, as written in Luke 12:7, God knows the count of every strand of hair on your head. The bottom line is that he wants us to get to know him personally, and the way to do that is by spending time with him. Successful relationships are built on time, and God wants time with you.

This chapter will teach you how to spend quality time with God, getting you closer to him and in his presence. In his presence, prayers are answered, and healing takes place. First things first, I want to make a point that religion is different from relationship. People get hung up on religion when you ask them about their relationship with God. You will hear, "Yes, I have a relationship with God, I attend Pastel Missionary Baptist, or Roger Pentecostal, so on and so forth. There are nearly 37 million churches in the world of all different denominations, but getting in the presence of God takes more than a Sunday attendance. Most people don't read their Bible, worship God, nor pray unless they are in church. I want to make the distinction because people tend to approach God with a religious mindset by doing what they have seen others do or say. You must make your time with God personal, or your prayers will become ritualized, and you will find yourself saying the same thing every time that you pray. When you build a relationship with God, your prayer life shifts, it will become a more intimate conversation. This is when you can sit and tell God what is on your heart. As believers, once you have given your life to Christ, you become a child of God. *1 John 3:1 tells us that The Father has loved us so much that we are called children of God. Hebrew 4:16 reads Let us therefore come boldly to the throne of grace that we may obtain mercy and find grace to help in time of need.*

To build a relationship with God, we must first get to know him. When you first meet someone that you are interested in, you want to know everything about them, their favorite foods, colors, vacation locations, etc. Getting to know God is just as important, you get to know God by reading his Word through daily devotion with him then meditating on his Word. Meditation over the years has represented a negative connotation, that believers should not meditate. Contrary to what most believers have been told, the Bible demonstrates the importance of meditating in several scriptures in both the old and new testaments.

Josh 1:8 reads, Keep this book of the law always on your lips, meditate on it day and night, so that you may be careful to do everything written in it. Then you will be prosperous and successful. That scripture is profound and answers the questions of many, including myself. God gives us the answers to life mysteries through his Word. You may be thinking well, I read my bible app daily but listen that is not enough. You must sit and meditate on it to hear what God is trying to tell you for that day and at that moment. When you are reading your daily devotion, don't just read it and keep moving. Sit with it, read the commentary, search the reference scriptures, then think about what the scriptures are saying to you. You will find that even scriptures that you have read before will start to speak to you in your current state, you will begin to have a new understanding of what you have read and heard before.

Now that you've gotten a portion of the foundation of building a relationship with God by getting to know him through his Word, I want us to go deeper by getting into his Glory. Remember, I said that we were created for God's pleasure. It is true! We were created to worship God, but don't get confused because worship is different from praise. We tend to praise God very well. Praise is when we thank God for what he did, "Lord thank you for waking me up this morning, thank you for my job, etc.", Worship is thanking God for who he is when you have a light bill due and don't know how you are going to pay the bill and when you received a bad doctors report. You feel like everything is falling apart, and you tell God that you know that he is in control and can give him Glory even before it is finished.

Listening to worship music can help you to focus and not be distracted during your quiet time with God, but it is not required. Although it is not required, I recommend that you start your quiet time with worship music to help set the atmosphere. The cherubim or angels closest to God are constantly worshiping him. Isaiah 6:3 tells us that they are calling out to one another holy, holy, holy is the Lord of hosts; the whole Earth is full of his Glory. John 4:24 speaks about God being a spirit and that they that worship must worship him in spirit and in truth. This scripture is from the parable about the woman at the well who was thirsting for the wrong things. Jesus ultimately was able to get her to believe that with him, she would never thirst again. The same way that God did it for her, he can and will do it for you, through his presence.

There are levels to his presence, and I am sure that you think that yes, I have truly been in and felt the presence of God on Sundays while I got my shout on all over the church; that was a good word, but still, you remain unchanged. Being in the presence of God is not about emotional worship, ritualistic Sunday services, nor religious prayers.

The presence is intimacy with God, period. When we come before God with clean hands and a pure heart, no longer trusting in idols (those things that we put before God that are false gods, looking to other things for answers instead of God), he is there and ever-present with you.

Knowing that God is present requires that you increase your consciousness. How might you ask? You must allow your thinking to be focused on him all day. If you do this, God promises to keep you in perfect peace, whose mind stays on him. To increase, you must practice his presence so that you experience him. When you are studying the Word, you are practicing his presence. Whatever you are exposed to the most is what you will think about the most. You must think about what you are focused on every moment. The more that you are exposed to the presence of God, the easier it is for you to break through and begin to experience him. There is something about exposure; for example, take a fruit tree that has been planted if it is exposed to the sunlight and water it will bear fruit effortlessly. So, if you, as a believer, would expose yourself to the (son-life) and the water of his Word, you will begin to bear fruit effortlessly.

Psalm 16:11 (NKJV) says, You will show me the path of life; In Your presence is fullness of joy; At Your right hand are pleasures forevermore. That's what I have been desiring, to be face to face with God, at his feet soaking up his Glory.

his Glory. You know God as much as you know his Word, which meant that I needed to study to increase my passion and hunger for more of God. As I began to spend more time with God, I realized that it helped rid distractions, and my time with him became more intimate. As the atmosphere shifted, that's when I began to release and humble myself to hear.

Do you feel God near, while you worship, while you meditate on his Word and while you read the Word? What is he saying to you on this day? If you have an ear to hear, receive the Word from God, then write.

CHAPTER 2

Hearing from God

Hearing from God through prayer is a two-way conversation. Prayer is having a personal conversation with God, and it is not rushed. You can't do all the talking and don't allow God the chance to speak back. Have you ever had a conversation with a friend and they monopolized the entire conversation? Right! You can never get a word in, you can walk away from the phone, come back, and they never knew that you left. Listen, please don't cheat God; we must talk to him the same way that we speak to our closest friends, then sit in a quiet place and allow him the opportunity to talk back. Philippians 4:6 tells us to be anxious for nothing but in everything by prayer and petition with thanksgiving, present your requests to God. As you build your relationship with God, the more intimate you will become with him, the more you will feel his closeness, and you will notice a shift in your prayer life. It is essential to understand that when you accepted Jesus as your savior, you became part of the family of God. As part of the family, you have access to allow God to lead and direct your path. Is that what we all want to hear from God?

Hearing doesn't require you to beg and plead, only to ask, then listen. God is right there waiting for you to talk to him so that he can speak back. Communication is vital to your relationship with God, and being in his presence takes time. The relationship that you desire from God that includes the closeness where you hear from him when he speaks requires intimate time with him. You will notice that as you begin to do this, you will start to feel a pull or unction from God to spend time with him when you have not made yourself available. Being in his presence helps you to understand why God would meet with Adam in the garden. He wants the same from you, to draw you to the secret place of the most high. Psalm 91, teaches us that God wants you to dwell with him and when you dwell, that means to stay there, spend time with him in his secret place, that can only be found in his presence. When you hear from God, you hear through your spirit, not your mind, emotions, nor your flesh. God speaks to the spirit that lives within us.

Our approach to listening to God comes with you having the ability to hear with clarity and understand how he speaks today. God speaks in different ways and to each person differently. He speaks to you according to your personality. The primary way that God speaks is through his Word as you study and meditate on it to hear exactly what he is trying to say to you in a still small voice that people often interpret as a gut feeling. Have you ever been driving over the speed limit, and something says you better slow down, and then there is a police officer nearby? Listen to that voice; it's not just your gut; it's the spirit man directing you. Being able to hear God speak to us becomes a way of life if you are communicating or praying regularly. When you do, subconsciously, we should always be listening, allowing ourselves to be sensitive to the spirit. When you have a listening spirit, you make it a priority by:

1. learning to listen

2. Pursuing it by increasing your study time with God

3. Being persistent, making sure that you do it regularly

4. Prayer asking God to teach you how to hear from him

When you develop a more in-depth, closer relationship with God, you will demonstrate five distinguishable characteristics. To effectively hear from God, you must have a Teachable Spirit, open and acknowledging the need to learn. Ask yourself, do you want to know more? Secondly, you need to have an Attentive Spirit, taking the time to concentrate and be still allowing yourself to hear from God. The Holy Spirit will manifest himself when we are; still, stillness activates his power. Being still may be a challenge because you're sitting and doing nothing. Psalm 40:1 reads, I waited patiently, and he inclined to me and heard my cry. Proverbs 4:20-22 says, Son, give attention to my words: incline your ear to my sayings. Do not let them depart from your eyes; Keep them in the midst of your heart; For they are life to those who find them, and health to all their flesh. Thirdly, you need to have a humble spirit by acknowledging the need to learn. A submissive spirit according to Deuteronomy 11:13 it shall be that if you earnestly obey my commandments which command you today, to love the Lord your God and serve him with all your heart and with all your soul. The point is, why should God even speak to you if you are not willing to listen to what he has to say. Finally, you need an expectant spirit Proverbs 8:34; Blessed is the man who listens to me, watching daily at my gates, waiting at the post of my doors. When you pray and ask God for something, his Word says to expect it and remind God daily. God's Word is true and will not be returned to him void, meaning that we serve a God that cannot and will not lie. The deeper you get in his presence, you will become stronger in areas where you have been weak and find that your flesh will start to lose the grip that it has had on you.

When you are in his presence, you may find yourself singing a song of praise and don't even realize it, often swaying back and forth. It is truly a beautiful intimate place to be where God can speak to you. While God is speaking, start to journal. I recommend that you begin your time with God with a journal, pen, Bible, and worship music ready to go. As you sit still, begin to write whatever you feel your heart is saying. Don't worry about it making sense, just write. You will find that God is speaking to your heart and transcribing on paper. Make sure to date your journal entries as God will prove his Word to be true. One day you will be able to look back into your journal and read the confirming Word.

Take this time to think about what you have read and your thoughts. Below are some additional scriptures for your reading and further study.

John 10:27 My sheep hear my voice, and I know them, and they follow me.

Romans 10:17 So faith comes from hearing, and hearing through the Word of Christ. (How do we hear – through the Word by reading the scripture.

Jeremiah 33:3 Call to me and I will answer you and will tell you great and hidden things that you have not known. (God speaks to you – through two-way communication) Where intimacy of communion exists God will answer the call of his own, that follow him.

John 8:47 Whoever is of God hears the words of God. The reason why you do not hear them is that you are not of God. (Salvation Required – follow God).

Isaiah 30:21 And your ears shall hear behind you, saying this is the way, walk in it, when you turn to the right or when you turn to the left. (God will give you directions when he speaks to walk out your day. Come from under financial hardship, create wealth, multiple streams of income.

John 16:13 When the spirit of truth comes, he will guide you into all truth, for he will not speak on his own authority but whatever he hears he will speak, he will declare to you the things that are to come.

Luke 11:28 But he said, Blessed rather are those who hear the Word of God and keep it. (obedience to God — hearing and doing)

Is God speaking to you at this moment? Have you set aside time for him, or are you doing a drive-by for Jesus? He is not fast food. Time with him is a five-course meal; it takes time. Give him time today and receive his direction. As he speaks, write.

CHAPTER 3

Walking in the Fullness

Walking in the fullness of God's plan for your life, you must remember that your lifestyle can cause static and prevent you from adequately hearing from God. John 10:27 tells us that you, my sheep, hear my voice, and I know them, and they follow me. For God to know you means that you have accepted Christ as your savior and believe that Jesus died and rose on the third day. Salvation is key to God, knowing you. Follow is important here in this scripture as it is a verb that means to be a follower, a person who believes in a particular cause, faith, or person.

Walking in the fullness allows you to hear God's instructions and plans for your life. These plans and instructions can result in million-dollar ideas, new businesses, and how ways to improve your current business. The ideas may result in authoring books as I am doing at this moment, and even new inventions. God will give you a blueprint for your life.

Walking in the fullness allows you to give God complete control over your life. When you give God control, you are listening to the plans that he has for you. According to James 1:17, God will open your eyes, heart, and ears to the fact that everything good comes from God. Promotions and an increase in your jobs come from God. You must put God first, work unto him, and stop looking at a man. When increase and promotions happen, then you will know without a doubt that it came from God.

Walking in the fullness of God allows you to know the love of Christ firsthand and understand that there is strength in God's love. When you have one of those days where you need to press your way, according to Ephesians 3:14 that you have to pray for spiritual strength, for this reason, I bow my knees before the Father, from where every family in heaven and on Earth is named, that according to the riches of his glory he may grant you to be strengthened with power through his Spirit in your inner being, so that Christ may dwell in your hearts through faith that you, being rooted and grounded in love, may have the strength to comprehend with all the saints what is the breadth and length and height and depth, and to know the love of Christ that surpasses knowledge, that you may be filled with all the fullness of God.

Walking in the fullness of God reveals the secret to pleasures forevermore with hope for the future. God's blessings and direction isn't just a one-time thing. Relationships with God are forever. God doesn't leave us or turn his back on you, no matter what. This relationship is built on time and the closeness that you obtain through being in his presence. Psalm 24:1-6 The Earth is the Lords' and all its fullness, the world and those who dwell therein. For he has founded it upon the seas and established it upon the waters. Who may ascend into the hill of the Lord? Or who may stand in His holy place? He who has clean hands and a pure heart, who has not lifted up his soul to an idol, nor sworn deceitfully. He shall receive blessings from the Lord, and righteousness from the God of his salvation. This is Jacob, the generation of those who seek him, Who seek your face.

Breathe in the Peace of God and out, stress, and those things that pull you away from who he is in your life. Remember that God's Word is true. Walk-in his ways today and focus your mind on Jesus. Think of those things that are good and know that when you are ready to hear that God will speak. Is he talking to you today? Listen, then write.

CHAPTER 4

Listening to God

Are you getting distracted and believe you've done all the right things and still wondering if you are hearing from God? Well, there is only one requirement; the ability to listen to God is limited to believers. We hear from God through our spirt; we do not hear or listen through our minds, our emotions, nor our flesh. We hear from God through the Holy Spirit; he is the receiver. Now that you understand how to hear from God, it is important that you understand the approach to hearing from him. God speaks to your spirit in different ways. He speaks through a still small voice that is often mistaken as your own thoughts or a gut feeling. God speaks through his word, and the scriptures speak. As you sit and meditate on the word, you will find that you can read the same scripture again and again then get a completely different understanding out of what God wants to say to you at that moment. God also speaks through other people that you may or may not know. It is essential to know that when God speaks, it is encouraging and not condemning. God can also speak through circumstances that happen in our lives. We can go through a situation or circumstance that can change the course of your life. The primary way that God speaks is through his word. You must spend enough time meditating on his word. When someone tells you God said, you should be able to validate what they are telling you in his word. When someone gives you a word from God, to confirm they need to stay within the principles of scriptures.

Your ability to listen can be blocked by static caused by sin, which can interfere with you hearing the still small voice of God. Sin grieves the spirit and limits the spirit from hearing. We want to develop such a listening ear that hearing God speak should be like second nature and part of your day. Learning to listen should be a way of life. He is always speaking, and if you don't want to miss him, you need to be sensitive to the voice of God no matter where you are. You can be driving, walking, and even grocery shopping when he speaks, so have a listening ear and be ready to receive.

To be sensitive, you need to develop a listening spirit by making God a priority and learning to listen. Then you need to pursue God by studying the Word and meditating on it to see what he is saying to you. You can't just do this once it requires that you persist in it. Then pray and ask God to teach you how to hear from him when he speaks.

There are five characteristics you should develop if you truly want to hear from God.

1. You need to be teachable, open to God to teach you.

2. Attentive, taking the time to get quiet. Proverbs 4:20-21 My son, give attention to my words; incline your ear to my sayings. Do not let them depart from your eyes; keep them in the midst of your heart.

3. Humble, acknowledging the need to learn. Psalm 25:9 He leads the humble in what is right and teaches the humble his way.

4. Submissive, why should God speak if you are not going to obey. Deuteronomy 11:13 And if you will obey my commandments that I command you today, to love the Lord your God and to serve him with all your heart and with all your soul.

5. Expectant, you are anticipating what God is going to say. Proverbs 8:34 Blessed is the one who listens to me watching daily at my gates, waiting beside my doors. When you ask God for something, stay there and keep reminding him, expect it to happen.

Take time today to pray and ask God to speak; his servant is listening then write.

CHAPTER 5

Removing blockages

Removing any obstacles or static from your life is a necessity for clarity when you want to hear from God. No one is perfect, but God requires that we try. It is a process. Yes, we are covered by grace, but I view grace as one large umbrella. As long as you are under the umbrella, you are covered, but when you step out from under the covering, you expose yourself to the entrapment of the enemy. Romans 3:23 tells us that we have all sinned and fallen short of the glory of God. Sometimes we are unable to move forward because of the cyclical sin that requires that we remove ourselves from certain situations. Genesis 39:1-20 is a perfect example of moving yourself from certain situations.

In this chapter, we learn about Joseph, who was bought at a price and made a slave by the Egyptian Potiphar, an officer to Pharaoh. Joseph found himself alone with Potiphar's wife, who tried to seduce him. Joseph had to remove himself from the situation, and he fled from the house. He had to run for his life to get out of a situation, even leaving behind his coat. Joseph knew that this would have resulted in him committing adultery with another man's wife. Cyclical sins are more difficult because we become comfortable and repeat then over and over again to the point where you no longer feel convicted.

Living a life pleasing to God is where I desire to be. I understand that it is a process and that no one is perfect. Colossians 3 teaches us how to live a Christian life that focuses on how to remove sin by removing ourselves from sin. This is what Joseph had to do. For me, I've had to change and renew relationships. The places that I used to go to; I knew that I couldn't go to those places anymore. Removing yourself starts with where you put your focus. In this study guide, you have learned by being in the presence of God that our focus should be on the things of God. Colossians 3:1-2 (NIV) reads: Since then, you have been raised with Christ, set your heart on things above, where Christ is seated at the right hand of God. Set your minds on things above, not earthly things.

Changing the people around you is crucial. If you pay attention, you will notice that your attitude will reflect the people you surround yourself with. Even if you are trying to have a positive attitude, if you are surrounded by negativity, your temperament will be disrupted and take a downswing. Removing static requires that we replace our sinful nature with different options. God doesn't want you to stop living, but he does want all of you!

Below are some examples of how you can replace a sin nature:

Cover yourself with compassion — be concerned about what others may be going through.

Be kind — I try to think before I speak because I've had problems with controlling my temper.

Be gentle and patient — tolerate without becoming annoyed, having a mild temper.

Forgive others — think about those that you have not forgiven.

Be filled with love — God wants you to be complete in him, knowing that he loves you for who you are, and he wants us to love others in a way that it doesn't leave room for anything else.

Let the peace of God take charge — allow God to take over your worries, cast your cares on him. Allow God to carry you; let him carry the burden of life.

Let scriptures penetrate you deeply — meditate on the Word, sit with it, don't just read it, then move on. Ask what does the scripture means to me? What is it saying to you?

Worship God by singing to him with gratitude — every morning, make time for God; we were created to worship. Know that when you worship that God is present.

Finish Strong today, rest in the presence of God. Listen to what he is saying to you and write.

CHAPTER 6

Exercising Vision, By Letting Go!

Now that you have removed the static and obstacles from your life to move forward, you now need to let go. Remember Romans 3:23; we have all sinned and fallen short of the Glory of God. Often our shortcomings keep us from moving forward. Letting go means that you are starting fresh. Luke 5:37 tells us that no one puts new wine into old wineskins or else the new wine will burst and spill out.

God has a purposed plan for your life, but have you delayed the promise? Jeremiah 29:11 (NKJV) For I know the thoughts that I think toward you, says the Lord, thoughts of peace and not of evil, to give you a future and a hope. The plan already exists; it is what we do that delays the release. You need to exercise the vision, be determined about what you want to achieve. This determination requires that we spend time with God every single day. You should talk to God when your feet hit the floor, or even before you get out of the bed. Talking to God is not optional if you want to move forward now that you have let go. Once you get the static and obstacles out of the way, it now up to you. Therefore, you need to spend time with God when you feel like it, and when you don't. Start your day by letting the enemy know that his already defeated!

If you can only call on God when you are in church, the enemy knows that he can take you on, and delay your vision.

Listen, the enemy is not afraid of you only knowing God's presence in the church. He is afraid when you recognize God's presence everywhere you go, in your car, while washing dishes, while you're at work and even walking down the street. You want the enemy to be afraid, be very afraid. Tell him to back up off your vision! If you remain in God's presence, this will make it harder for him to stop the plans that God has for your life.

The point is you don't want anything or anyone keeping you from the promise. Mark 4:15 – 20 (NKJV) talks about being able to receive what God has for you and to prosper. It reads: And these are the ones by the wayside where the Word is sown. When they hear, Satan comes immediately and takes away the Word that was sown in their hearts. These likewise are the ones sown on stony ground who, when they hear the Word, immediately receive it with gladness; and they have no root in themselves, and so endure only for a time. Afterward, when tribulation or persecution arises for the Word's sake, immediately they stumble. Now, these are the ones sown among thorns; they are the ones who hear the Word, and the cares of this world, the deceitfulness of riches, and the desires for other things entering in choke the Word and becomes unfruitful. But these are the ones sown on good ground, those who hear the Word, accept it, and bear fruit: some thirtyfold, some sixty, and some a hundred. Versus 19 teaches us that distractions cause us to be unfruitful. When you have removed the stumbling blocks and let go of the things that continue to hold you back, you move from being unfruitful to fruitful and producing a harvest. Verse 20 is the fertile ground that's ready to produce a harvest. Don't you want to produce a harvest of 30, 60 or even 100 times? Bottom line you get what you put in and remember, it takes work.

Visions are blocked by damaged areas in our hearts, those footpaths that are hardened not easily penetrated. These are the areas in our lives where we no longer have faith to believe. Listen, we mustn't allow the enemy to steal, kill, and destroy God's plans for your life. To exercise vision, we must first surrender. It is God's will that we produce a harvest. John 15:16 (NKJV) You did not choose Me, but I chose you and appointed you that you should go and bear fruit and that your fruit should remain, that whatever you ask the Father in my name he may give you lasting fruit. The key to this scripture is lasting fruit. Having the right soil is paramount to proper planting if there will be a harvest. We want the fertile ground. Say it out loud, "I want a harvest!" We want to produce a harvest of thirty, sixty, and even one-hundred times what we put in!

Spend the time now, listening to the words that God wants you to receive. Write what you believe God is saying here.

CHAPTER 7

Celebrate the Wins!

Letting Go and exercising the vision that God has for your life requires that you first truly let go, we now know that we must get the static out of our lives. Static is referred to those things; obstacles that you need to Let Go and Get Over so you can move forward. As you read this chapter, I want you to Celebrate the Wins! Often we live our lives in condemnation and regret, thinking about what you did yesterday. I want you to know that we serve a God that does not focus on yesterday; he is a God of Today!

In this teaching, the book of Lamentations is relevant. To give you some background, if you've never read or heard of this book of the Bible, the Word Lamentations in the Greek means tears or wailings. This book refers to the fall of the tribe of Judah and the capture of Jerusalem, not to get too deep because I can only imagine the look on your face right now. Lamentations chapter 3 describes their suffering as a result of their sin and the judgment of God, but in vs. 21, the tribe of Judah is reminded of God's affection and were called to REPENT! Verse 22 reads Through the Lord's mercies we are not consumed, and his compassion fails not, or The Lord's kindness never fails! Verse 23 (NKJV) They are new every morning, Great is your faithfulness. Which means the Lord can always be trusted to show mercy each morning (CEV).

God is a forgiving God full of mercy, which leads me to John 8: 1-11, the parable or story about the woman accused of adultery. The story is found in John 8:1-11 (NKJV) But Jesus went to the Mount of Olives. Now early in the morning, He came again into the temple, and all the people came to Him; and He sat down and taught them. Then the scribes and Pharisees brought to Him a woman caught in adultery. And when they had set her in the midst, they said to Him, "Teacher, this woman was caught in adultery, in the very act. Now Moses, in the law, commanded us that such should be stoned. But what do You say?" This they said, testing Him, that they might have something of which to accuse Him. But Jesus stooped down and wrote on the ground with His finger, as though He did not hear. So, when they continued asking Him, He raised Himself up and said to them, "He who is without sin among you, let him throw a stone at her first." And again, He stooped down and wrote on the ground. Then those who heard it, being convicted by their conscience, went out one by one, beginning with the oldest even to the last. And Jesus was left alone, and the woman standing in the midst. When Jesus had raised Himself up and saw no one but the woman, He said to her, "Woman, where are those accusers of yours? Has no one condemned you?" She said, "No one, Lord." And Jesus said to her, "Neither do I condemn you; go and sin no ore more."

When reading these scriptures, people often stop at Jesus, saying that he does not condemn us, but he also says to go, which means to go, move forward, and don't look back. Sin No More! Similar to the woman being accused. I was raised to believe that every time that I did anything that "others" or my accusers like the woman in the story; said that I did wrong, that God was mad with me, and I was no longer saved because I had sinned. I was not taught that God doesn't condemn us and that he has compassion for us when we repent! In the book of John, we learn that Jesus, does not publicly address the woman about the sin that she was being accused of. In fact, he spoke to the accusers as if the woman was not there. Jesus only addresses the woman privately when it was only the two of them. He already knew that she had a repentant heart. John 2:25 teaches us that no one had to tell Jesus what people were like because he already knew.

Still, Jesus did not take her sin lightly; he commanded she go and sin no more. Listen, every day is a new day; we should be moving forward, celebrate the wins, when you're not committing the same sin over and over that is a win! Now, if you are, you need to go back and read the previous chapter. Romans 12:1 Teaches us to be transformed! Mathew 9:17 Ask why would you pour new wine into old wineskins when it only bursts, losing the wine. Therefore Go! Move forward and win in any area of your life where you struggle. Don't condemn yourself, repent, and remember that there are new mercies that await you!

> Like new wine, God wants to change you from the inside out!
>
> Celebrate the Wins!

We serve a loving God, and as we walk this walk of life, he doesn't expect us to be perfect but he does expect us to try! 2 Chronicle 16:9 (NKJV) tells us that God is looking for those whose heart is entirely his! As this chapter comes to an end, stop being hard on yourself as you study God's Word, he will transform your life. When you fall into sin, ask for forgiveness, and mean it. If you keep repeating the same sin, it means that you did not truly repent. No sins are greater than the other. Listen to your heart; it will tell when you should or should not do something. When you overcome, Celebrate the Win!

CHAPTER 8

Don't Give Up!

If you have been following along throughout the chapters, meditating, and listening to God, you need to know that it's not easy, but be thankful for the progress! You will never be perfect, but you should see changes in your life where you can say; I am NOT the person that I used to be! Your past is your past. Thank God for Lamentations 3:23 as we expounded teaches us that we have new mercies from God every day. Yes, New Mercies!

Listen, you have come this far; keep pushing; keep believing, keep pressing. God will answer your prayers. Matthew 15:21-28 (NKJV) Gives the example of the Canaanite woman's faith. This woman had a need, and she followed after Jesus and his disciples to the point where the disciples wanted to send her away, but Don't Give Up! She continued to press her way, begging Jesus to help her. To test her faith, Jesus tells her in verse 26 It is not meet to take the children's bread and cast it to the dogs.

The woman passed the test by not giving up! She replied, Lord, even the dogs eat from the crumbs which fall from their masters' table. Because she didn't give up, versus 28 says; That Jesus declared, O woman great is thy faith; be it done unto thee. She was rewarded with a miracle. Jesus answered her prayer.

So, I asked you? "What have you prayed and asked God for?" Remember, Isaiah 43:26 tells us to Put me, meaning

God, in remembrance of his Word that you may be justified. Your prayers will be answered.

Believe that God's Word is true, and it changes not. Don't give up on your Family; restoration is near. Don't give up on your Faith God will soon answer your prayers. Don't give up! The new job is on the way; I see the open doors that have been closed in your face. Don't give up on your business! Declare this is my year of growth. Remember Philippians 4:13 I can do All Things! Repeat to yourself again and again! I Can Do All Things! Let it marinate in your heart, and the Bible says All not Some! So, when you feel like quitting, remember, Don't Give Up!

Listen, you have come too far, to give up now. It is a process, and if you are making progress, Don't Give Up!

As these devotionals close, I want to take the time to pray with you as you forge forward, allowing God to transform your life. Allow him to renew your mind and change your thinking as you get to know him more intimately by spending time with him. You will find that you will begin to hear him more clearly. When God begins to speak, write what you hear, and feel in your heart. Before I pray, what is God saying?

Father in the Name of Jesus, today we stand on the word believe that every thing that you said will come to past in our lives. We believe in every promise an we will not Give Up! Amen.

CHAPTER 9

Prayer and Declaration

Father, thank you for the opportunity to be with you in your presence. We thank you, God, because we know that we are not alone and that you hear our prayers. As your children, we bring you in remembrance of your word. We come before you with humble and willing hearts. Search us and remove any influence, obstacle, distraction that's keeping us from fully surrendering to you. Thank you for renewed mercies today and that you hear our prayers. Wake up the dormant, dead places in our lives and supernaturally catapult us in the direction that you will have us to go. We declare that we will have renewed insight, a renewed focus that will complete unfinished visions and dreams.

We thank you that Psalm 84:11 says that if we live Right, that no good thing will you withhold from us. So, we arrest our flesh and stand under an open heaven. We thank you for not just what you do but who you are: A mighty God, A counselor, A friend, A burden barrier. You are omniscient (all-knowing), omnipotent (all power rest in your hands), and we give you Glory. As your children, we bring you in remembrance of your Word. I declare that every prayer request is being answered. I thank you that every obstacle, boundary, and limit placed on our lives that have held us back, held us up, prevented us from completing our goals, is being removed, destroyed, and demolished in Jesus' Name. Father, even when it seems like you are not going to answer our prayer or show up, we know that it all happens in your time, and we will not give up. We will hold on to the promise of your Word, ask, and you shall receive, knock, and the door will be opened. I declare supernaturally that right now as we pray that war angels are being dispatched to the heavens to fight the enemy that is holding up your answers. According to Mathew 16:19, We have been given keys whatever we bind on Earth will be loosed in heaven. We bind up financial drought; we lose financial overflow. We bind up broken homes and release restoration in families. We arrest our flesh and stand under an open heaven. Father speak into the lives of your sons and daughters let them know that you are with them and have not forsaken. I declare that every purposed plan for our lives will come alive in Jesus' Name. We take dominion over the things on this Earth. I declare that new and better jobs are coming, enlarged territories. Enemy, you are subject to the authority of God. Every plan and strategy that you have orchestrated we place under our feet. You can't have our children, and you can't have our minds, we will not be marginalized nor held back.

Today in your presence, we declare healing and declare that cancer is being dried up and any affliction that has attached itself to your physical body. Enemy, I say it again! Every planned obstacle, we crush right now under our feet. We destroy every wicked plan that you had for our lives and our family lives. We take back our joy, hope, peace today.

We will not give up and declare Victory in our life. Clean our lives from anything that displeases you, and that may keep you from full-fulling the plans that you have ordained for our lives. Wash our minds of carnality that our territories may be enlarged. Release everything that the enemy has illegally held back from us. I pray right now that the anointing of God will break every yoke of bondage. I pray that the angels assigned to you will stand guard over you daily as you advance to new levels, new dimensions, and new territories. I saturate the atmosphere and declare that every piece of your destiny is coming together. I believe right now for new wine that everything is working according to God's will. We tear down and break every barrier. You are advancing right now on a level playing field with wisdom, new strategies, and divine tactics we praise you, God, that you are leading the way.

Holy Spirit, we give you complete access to our mind, soul, and spirit. I declare that every mountain in your life has been made low. You are advancing pass stubborn problems and situations or anything that will stand in the way of my progress. I no longer walk in fear according to Psalm 23:4 yea though I walk through the valley; I will fear no evil because you are with me! We let go of all worries, and thank you that closed doors are now being opened. Thank you for healing damaged hearts that have been broken, disappointed and have been walked over. Fill their hearts with new love, increase our desire to exercise the vision, and the plans that you have for our lives. Thank you for helping us walk this thing out that we call life from day to day. As we go forth, we walk in freedom, knowing that you are with us. Thank you that we can call you and you will answer. We give you thanks, Father, we give you Glory and count this prayer done, finished in Jesus' Name!

CHAPTER 10

It's Time to Shift!

For nearly three months we have been shut up, quarantined, and required to social distance from those that we love. As I began to ask God what is next? He gave me one word for the month: SHIFT! It means to move or cause to move from one place to another, a slight change in position, direction in tendency. When you look at tendency it refers to how you would normally do something.

Today, I want you to know that it is no longer business as usual. God wants you to SHIFT. Being quarantined is like being in a cave with no access to the norm but God is shaking things up. I am reminded by Lazarus in John 11:1-44 (NKJV)

[1]Now a certain man was sick, Lazarus of Bethany, the town of Mary and her sister Martha. [2]It was that Mary who anointed the Lord with fragrant oil and wiped His feet with her hair, whose brother Lazarus was sick. [3]Therefore the sisters sent to him, saying, "Lord, behold, he whom You love is sick."

[30]Now Jesus had not yet come into the town but was in the place where Martha met him. [31]Then the Jews who were with her in the house, and comforting her, when they saw the Mary rose up quickly and went out, followed her, saying, "She is going to the tomb to weep there."

Jesus was friends with Lazarus, Martha, and Mary of Bethany (Lazarus' sisters), but when he was told that that Lazarus was sick; everyone expected Jesus to show-up and heal him! This time Jesus responded differently, he waited and waited; four days passed and by this time Lazarus was not only dead, but he had been placed in a cave or tomb for four days. Jesus changed his tendency and did the opposite of what he would have normally done. Why, because Jesus had to SHIFT!

It was time for him to move and operate at new levels. This new level, the SHIFT resulted in Jesus showing up and asking where they have buried Lazarus. He then said roll the stone away! Then declared; Lazarus come forth and as he spoke those words he came out of the grave, no doubt hoping because he was bound in grave clothes with his hands and feet tied! He also has a napkin tied around his face… *(with the current pandemic does that sound familiar, as we walk around with masks on our face?)* The same way that Jesus said Lazarus come forth… He is calling you to-day. There are some dead dreams dormant in your life that God is calling out! There are books and businesses that he is saying come forth when we come out of this quarantine.

In order to come forth you must; **1) SHIFT your mind-set.** Instead of thinking about what you do not have, start walking like the heir to the throne. Psalm 84:11 For the Lord

God is a sun and shield. The Lord bestows grace and favor and honor. "No good thing will he withhold from those who walk uprightly." You should come out of the cave/quarantine better than you went in. I believe God is birthing Greatness during this time. **2) SHIFT your time management.** Instead of having idle time, finish something that you have started. Start something that been pending, create something that you have been dreaming about. Do not waste time, do something productive with it. **3) SHIFT your finances.** All the money that you would be spending hanging out on the town, traveling, shopping or even getting your hair cut for the men or styled for the women. Use it wisely and Pay off your debt!

Lazarus was bound and Jesus set him free! He commanded that the grave clothes lose him and let him go! God wants the same for you... to Come Out *BETTER, WISER, RENEWED, RE-ENERGIZED* and *RE-ENGAGED* to accomplish the purpose plan that God has for your life!

I leave you with this as you close this devotional. We will NOT return to normal So Get Ready for the New Normal!

SHIFT!

CHAPTER 11

Release It!

As we continue in Quarantine our country is yet faced with another Crisis! We can not take lightly what we see happening around us during this painful time in history. Black Lives Matter!! Yes, we believe that all lives do matter but in this time we are focused on the pain that we African Americans continue to face time after time that have caused an uproar not only in the USA but all around the world.

God gave me one word for this month, RELEASE! With all the pain that is languishing in the land, circulating in media there is no secret that people are angry, fed-up, and crying out for help. The patterns of practice that we continue to see will no longer be tolerated and has begun to spill out into uncontrolled emotions. People are even beginning to ask, "Where is God?"

I am remined of Isaiah 43:2 (NLT)

[1]Throughout everything it is important to know that God is there even in the battles!

Yes, God is even there thru the battles because sometimes we will have to stand-up for ourselves and fight for injustice but remember when doing so, we need to use wisdom!

Deuteronomy 20:1-4 Talks about the laws concerning war.

It is clear that the enemy is REAL and will stop at nothing and you better know that he is angry! It is important to know that this is a spiritual war!

Listen, we first entered to into a world-wide shut down due to a viral pandemic COVID-19 and as a result people across the Globe began to cry out to God and pray. People that have never prayed before! As the numbers started to decline and areas were slowly starting to re-open, we were attacked again.

Now, we have yet another senseless death! If you are paying close attention you would see that the accused officer that performed this injustice had the face of someone being controlled by a dark, demonic murderous spirit. Which has now incited uncontrolled riots and rage that have multiplied like never in history.

Unfortunately, as crowds gather, we must prepare for a rise in COVID again! We must stay in prayer that the enemy does not rise up against our younger generation that are fighting for the injustice in justice. This generation has taken a stance on their beliefs both spiritual and political. They have decided to have a voice and that they will no longer stand for it!

Today, I want to remind you that you do not have to face this alone, nor fight this battle by yourself. Realize that God is Greater than any circumstance that you will face. He fights for us!

I know that it does not feel like it because we are in the heat of battle and everyone is rising up because history has demonstrated that sometimes this is what it takes. For example, after Dr. Martin Luther King Jr. died in 1968 his assassination caused riots. The King Assassination riots, was also known as the Holy Week Uprising a wave of civil disturbance that spread across the United States. This wave of unrest was worse than the what the country experienced since the Civil War. Consequently, this resulted in the Civil Rights Act allowing for equal housing based on race, and religion. Even after this, today racism continues to spread and yes, we are still fighting!

Right now, as you are reading your heart and mind is trying to decide how to deal with the emotions that you are feeling (anger, rage, discontentment, and loss of peace). Your emotions are like a bottle that has been shaken up and is ready to explode but God is telling you to RELEASE IT! *Set it free, allow your emotions to escape confinement.*

Psalm 68:19 Tells us that:
God is the burden bearer.

You cannot keep the emotions confined because it is now attacking you! The body reacts to negatively when you hold on to anger and hurt, it begins to stop your body's ability to repair mechanisms which cause increase inflammation and the stress hormone!

So... RELEASE IT!

Do not make yourself sick...

COVID is still REAL and so is the ENEMY. God wants us to use wisdom and know that he is with you. It is important to pray and cover those that are taking a stand and protesting to stop the violence.

As we begin to dig deeper and look at where we currently are in time and what has happened historically. Ask the question, "What is God saying." Praying and seeking God allows me to see that there was a real significance to the word RELEASE. Dealing with the pain and anguish I began to ask God, "When will this end and God why us?" When I began to see the timeline of RELEASE come together as a prophetic roadmap to the plan that can only be orchestrated by God.

Our situation today is very similar to the what the children of Israel went through. They were also enslaved, mistreated, overworked and bound for 400 years and this year 2020, the year of double portion, double blessings marks the 400th year when the first slave stepped foot on the American soil. God is saying its time for our RELEASE. The life as we have lived is changed by the hands of times, God's hands that is. The death of George Floyd is now being used as a catalyst of change turning the hearts of those that have kept this generation of African Americans bound for centuries. Now this has become a united Global demand to stop the violence and bring recognition to, "Black Live Matter"!

This year, has been symbolic of a God's prophetic road-map since the first time in 2000 years we were behind closed doors, shut in like the children of Israel during Passover as the death angel spread throughout Egypt. Similar, the COVID virus spread throughout the land causing over 100 thousand deaths. The children of Israel were covered by the blood of a lamb that they crucified where we are covered by the precious lamb of God, Jesus Christ that was crucified for us.

In Exodus when God was preparing to RELEASE the children of Israel from the captivity, out of the hands of the Egyptians who had enslaved them, it did not come without a fight. When they departed, the Egyptians followed close behind, the children of Israel feared that they would be captured and returned as they approached the Red Sea.

But God Was There!

God parted the Red Sea and made a way for them when they could not see a way like what he is doing today! The world is uniting with millions marching for justice. How exciting it was to witness the streets of Paris filled with people wanting Justice for George Floyd and chatting, "Black Lives Matter."

Change is before us like never before. The hands of time are changing, and God's hands are busy at work. God is about to bring about a RELEASE, a turnaround to what we have been facing for 400 years. We are about to walk into our Promise this year, 2020! It is our time; it is our Season of RELEASE!

CHAPTER 12

Get Your Blessing

CoAuthor Daron Kuhn

Over the past month, God has begun leading us in a new direction that is more personal allowing us to deal with the shifting times that we are in, wearing mask and being away from our loved ones. During this time God has been drawing us closer to him and God is reminding us today that our 2020 visions have not expired and that is promises are YES and Amen! In this chapter we will focus on Getting your Blessing with a special guest Daron Kuhn.

We start with a passage from the bible Matthew 9:27 (New King James Version); When Jesus departed from there, two blind men followed him, crying out and saying, "Son of David, have mercy on us!". Jesus was approached by two bind men calling out for healing. Jesus touched their eyes and by faith Jesus said, "Let it be done on to you". Jesus healed the blind men and they went to spread the good news that once they were blind now, they see! Go Get your Blessing, like the two blind men. There are key principals on how to Get Your Blessings.

First, it is important to note in that the blind men follow but how do you follow when you cannot see? Someone around them was calling out the name Jesus. You must speak the name Jesus and surround yourself with likeminded, positive people that will uplift and encourage you. As a result, they were able to follow the voices by faith and then cried out to Jesus, "Have mercy on us Son of David". In other words, they were saying we need you more than ever, but Jesus ignored them. Do not be discouraged at the first response, you will have trials but do not stop, you must keep going and do what God has called you to do in this season. The blind men continued to press their way until they made it, from the outside to the inside of the house where Jesus was. So, do not give up and allow the enemy to discount what God is about to do in your life. You will have trials and will have to fight on every side. You will go through opposition and that typically means that something is about to happen for you. If God does not answer you the first time it does not mean that he has not heard your cry. When the men got in the inside Jesus asked, "Do you believe?" Jesus was pushing them toward faith. Faith is the currency that you need, to withdraw anything from God. You are closer to your blessing than you think, do not give up. Sometimes you will have to go from the outer court to the inner courts to get what you need from God. By any means necessary, you must tell yourself, I am going to do what I need to obtain what God has for me in this season.

Five Key points to help you Get Your Blessing:

1. **Pray and Prepare:** In this season, faith without works are dead. Prayers are not enough. You must do something. You cannot be complacent; you must stand up to the enemy and not allow him to take advantage of you. You must prepare, pray, and move to the place that God has for you.

2. **Know who you are:** God did not waste anything on you. If you are going to go after your blessing, what God has called you to do, you got to know that you are enough, blessed and determined.

3. **You must be dressed right dressed:** Ready to hear the command of God. God does not speak in a loud voice he whispers. You do not want to miss what God is doing in your life. You want to hear what God is saying. You must be on the right frequency.

4. **Do not lowball yourself:** know your worth. Know who you are in God and his promises in your life. In this season, you have to walk strong and know who you are in God. Recently, I was positioned to negotiate, and I prepared and told them why I deserved the salary that I was requesting. Despite the amount, I did not back down and later they sent an email saying accepted. God is about to do the same for you. He is

about to accept something that you have been waiting for by opening doors and clearing the path! Hang in there... Whatever you have been waiting for God to do in your life, do not give up faith because he is about to do it suddenly.

5. **Grasp the walk of favor:** God is leaning in your direction. Favor with God is better than money or anything else the world has to offer.

You are closer than you think. In 2019 you may have fumbled the ball, but God is about to do something miraculous in your life and give you the power to recover and touch down so Go Get Your Blessing! At the end of the text about the blind men it says that Jesus touched their eyes and now they can see. You need to know that when you are going after your blessing you often cannot see what God is doing in your life because it does not always come at a highpoint. Even in the times when it seems that every day we are in the valley, you must know that God is still God. He is still in the blessing business. Do not allow what is going on to distract you from what God is doing in your life.

By Faith, go after what God is calling in you to do; By Faith go after that business deal. Earlier this year Daren had to take a pharmacology class and found it difficult, he had to memorize 1000 words. He explained how, he was doubting himself and was not speaking faith. You must speak faith in this season. By Faith, he received an A!

Do not let the enemy come after your blessing like the widowed Shulamite woman in the bible that had lost everything, she had in 2 Kings 4, the debt collector had no additional belongings that they could take from her and decided to go after her children. Can you imagine someone coming after your child, your dreams, the very thing that you have cried over and sewn into trying to crush your vision. The Shulamite woman encounters the prophet Elisha and falls at his feet asking for help. Elisha gave her instructions, he asked, "what do you have in your house" and she replied, "a little oil". Elisha told her to go borrow all the jars that she could find, then go in the house and close the door and begin filling them with the oil. The bible says that the oil flowed until the jars ran out. She asked Elisha what she should do next and he told her go pay off your debt and for her and her sons to live off the rest!

The blessing was right there, in her hands and God is saying the same thing to you. The blessing is in your hands, the blessing is in your house! I pray that God will give you the same strength to Go Get Your Blessing. The Shulamite woman had to take first step to get her blessing. She had to knock on the doors, speak to request the jars, then filled them. It was a process!

You too must know that God is calling you to do something that you have never done before and that the blessing is in your hands, mouth and in your house. What does it mean inside your house, you might ask? Well God, has put something on the inside of you a book, or even a business. God has no respect of a person. God is saying that whatever you put your hands too in this season will be blessed. David had something in his house and yes, he was an adultery and a murderer, but God still blessed him. Even Moses, another murderer had something in his hands and something in his mouth that God used to bless the Egyptians. Let us not forget Esther who had something in her mouth and something in her house that liberated generations.

This is your time for the latter rain!

God wants to take you to new dimensions, new levels with open doors and renewed blessing. Like the blind men and the widowed Shulamite woman, By Faith you must believe and received it. I close this chapter by reminding that it is YOURS! Trust God in this season... Go Get Your Blessing! God is telling you that it is in your hands, your mouth and in your house!

CHAPTER 13

The Promises of God

As we enter the 8th month of the year and the number 8 stands for new beginnings. The last 7 months of this year has been life changing for us all... Good and at times bleak with so many uncertainties. Looking back over the past months teaching in May; God gave us one word, **SHIFT** with the quarantine it was important that we all make a change in how we would normally do things.

We discussed 3 points:

1. **We said that we need to <u>SHIFT</u> our mindset.**

2. **<u>SHIFT</u> our time management.**

3. **<u>SHIFT</u> our finances.**

This word carried us into June where through all the chaos, confusion and discontentment God said to **RELEASE IT** because not only were we dealing with a pandemic to include hatred that has been widespread and now have incited protest all over the world. This came with an entirely new set of uncertainties and emotions but remember God said **RELEASE IT** and give it to him!

As we enter into July, our guest minister Daron Kuhn reminded us that we were still in the year of Double, Double and to **Go Get your Blessings**! Despite the despair of what you see. There were 5 key points as noted below:

1. Pray and prepare.

2. Know who you are.

3. You must be dressed right dressed.

4. Do not low ball yourself.

5. Grasp the walk of Favor.

The key points were based on Matthew 9:27 where two blind men followed after Jesus with expectations. Expectations aligns with Faith!

When you look at the word Faith it means to have complete trust! It is the absence of doubt and for some of us including myself have been waiting for God's promises to be fulfilled!

This takes us finally to the moral of the teaching for this chapter; **"The Promises of God"**. First you must understand the basics, it may seem elementary, but it is important that we establish a foundation for your understanding. A promise is declaration or assurance that a particular thing will happen. The bible references the word promise 5467 times. It is important to note that God's promises are irrevocable! If you know that God has made a promise to you, then know that he is absolutely trustworthy. According to Numbers New King James Version (NKJV) 23:19 God is not a man, that he should lie, nor a son of man that he should repent. Has he said, and will not he not do?

If God says it, know that he is unchanging Psalm (NKJV) 110:4 The Lord has sworn and will not relent... God will not abandon his promise. You might be shedding tears right now and cannot understand what God is doing but I want you to know that God has the Power and will fulfill his promises. According to Isaiah (NKJV) 55:1, So Shall My word be that goes forth from My mouth; It shall not return to Me void, But is shall accomplish what I please, And it shall prosper in the thing for which I sent it! The scripture is confirming that God is Faithful in keeping his promises. When you look at the children of Israel in Joshua 21:45 not one promise failed.

I want to bring you focus to 7 promises:

1. God promises to be with you; Joshua (NKJV) Have I not commanded you? Be Strong and of good courage; do not be afraid, nor be dismayed, for the Lord your God is with you wherever you go. Also note Psalm (NKJV) 145:18-19 The lord is near to all who call on him in truth and Isaiah (NKJV) 12:2 Surely God is my salvation; I will trust and not be afraid.

2. God will protect you; Psalm (NKJV) 3:3-4 But you, O Lord are a shield for me, My glory and the One who lifts up my head! Another translation that touches my heart is from the Messenger version (MSG), I cried to the Lord with my voice and he heard me from his Holy Hill.

3. God will strengthen you; in times when we have all been tired, fed up and you may feel like you have lost momentum... Your plans and dreams have been stalled. But God! Psalm (NKJV) 46:1 God is our refuge and strength, A very present help in trouble.

4. God will Answer you; The answer might be Yes, or No and even sometimes Maybe then even Wait, which we do not want to hear. No matter the answer it is important to know that he WILL answer!

    I John New Living Translation (NLT) 5:14-15 And we are confident that he hears us whenever we ask for anything that pleases him. And since we know he hears us when we make our requests, we also know that he will give us what we ask for.

5. God will Provide for you; As we grow in God, we also grow in Gratitude for his blessings and we need to trust God even when things start to shift in a negative way we must believe that God will provide. As we set the course today, I declare over your life that according to Philippians (NKJV) And my God shall supply all your need according to His riches in glory by Christ Jesus!

6. God will give you Peace; This is precious because Peace is a gift from God that involves a wonderful feeling of well-being that reminds us that all is well

when Jesus is with us! John 16:33 tells that when you accept Christ in your life, he will give you peace as it says, In me you may have peace.

7. God will always love you! ALWAYS is key here and pierced my heart. No matter what we have done or what stage we are in our walk with Christ he is forgiving and will never stop loving you. Romans (NKJV) 8:31-31 says, if God is for you who can be against you!

There is a clear example that was provided to remind us all of God's promises and everyone can say that they have witnessed this in their life. The beautiful rainbow... Yes, that represents a promise from God. When God destroyed the earth in Genesis chapters 6-7 and asked Noah to build an ark and everyone thought that he was crazy. As the animals came and was gathered two of each kind, when the flood waters dried up and the only survivors were those on the Ark, Noah's family and the animals... God Promised not to destroy the earth again and the rainbow represents that promise to me and you today. Every time you see a rainbow, I want you to remember "The Promises of God", Yes, he is a Promise Keeper!

CHAPTER 14

Positioned to Push

Walk into the new timing a due time the month that represents a newness in life, birthing of goals, dreams, and aspirations. When a woman conceives it takes 4 trimesters before she travels to bring forth purpose and promise. This is the same as your purpose and promise. Like a woman you must be positioned to PUSH to deliver and birth a baby. In this chapter you will learn that being positioned to PUSH is key to move you into your purpose!

Ask yourself, are you moving into purpose? Why, because birthing has a due time and you do not want to miss your timing. You should be birthing new witty ideas planted in you by God, goals that you have set for yourself to achieve and the generations of promises that have been stored up in heaven. Yes, heaven has a storehouse for seeds sown through generations that can be reaped by you. Your due time harvest/birthing can be plentiful and dependent on the seeds sown. Some women give birth to one child at a time whereas there are others that may have twins, triplets, quadruplets and even more... Are you pregnant with multiple opportunities? Remember all things are possible through Jesus Christ according to Luke 1:37.

God wants you to bring forth and to do so God requires that you PUSH! Move into your purpose and come out of any stagnant place that you may have found yourself, making excuses for not finishing your goals, finishing your witty ideas... Do not miss out on your due season its your time to PUSH!

If you have found yourself stagnant in a dead unmotivated place that you have allowed yourself to be in, then you are sitting on gifts and ideas that God has given you but... Your due time has come, you can not wait any longer. Listen when a woman's time comes, she can not hold back the Birthing Process.

This process happens in three stages:

- **A woman will start to feel cramps and back pain in the natural that increase over time.**

- **She then feels like it is her time because the urge to PUSH is strong and she can no longer hold back that which is purposed to be here!**

Like the woman your purpose when it is your time places you in an uncomfortable state of discontentment, especially when you know that that God has given you an idea, task and you have not completed it but have been sitting on your gifting. It is important to note that everyone has a time and season to seize the moment and it is your divine time to act and do what God has placed on our heart.

But Are You READY?

God is calling you in this moment while you are reading this devotion to bring forth. Isaiah 66:7-9 New Living Translation (NLT) says, before she travailed, she brought forth; before her pain came, she was delivered of a man child...

Giving birth without pain is practically unheard of. God is trying to tell you in this season that what he is about to bring forth will amaze the onlookers as they wonder how did you do it... not believing that something of this sort could happen for you, that you cannot possibly have accomplished that. Not only will God blow your mind but the minds of those watching from afar on your social media pages, who secretly never supported you but now will see the harvest/birthing of your PUSH!

In this devotional there are three things that you need to have in place to bring forth:

    1. You must be in the right position.

    2. You must have the right posture.

    3. You must make the necessary preparation.

If you put these three things in place it will move you into your purpose and like the Isaiah 66 woman; you will give birth to purpose without pain.

The RIGHT position is key as being in the wrong will cause delay and unnecessary trial that you cannot avoid. Like a woman in the wrong birthing position can cause undue pain and injury that will take a long time to recover from!

Naturally before a baby is born it must turn in the right position! Being Positioned means that you must carefully place yourself in the right place. When you are in the right place it will be very difficult for you to miss God!

We are talking about being Positioned to Push, there is no time to lose focus while you are moving into your purpose. The plan for your life and purpose began before your mother new your father. God has a purposed plan for your life. According to Jeremiah 1:5 NLT, before God formed you, He knew you!

Therefore, before the seed was even planted in your mother's womb and fertilized by your father God said… Guess what ___________________ (make it personal), I know the plans that I have for you. I ordained you a *prophet*, I ordained you a *doctor*, a *lawyer*, a *chef*, a *judge*… Let God speak to you in the place where you are destined to be.

Knowing now that God established your purpose, there is no excuse. If you are not moving and walking in your purpose, it is because of you. God in all his sovereignty will not interfere in your will, you still must do the work.

God gives us choices and daily he gives us opportunities and options, it is up to you to be in the right POSTURE and POSTION!

When I say posture, I am not referring to how someone stands. To be in the right Posture means the approach you take to having the right attitude. This is interpreted by how you approach and deal with matters and situations.

This is where your preparation matters!

Even a woman prepares to birth; she learns to breath and to push through the pain without quitting. For example, let us look at the life of David and how he started out a sheep header. I Samuel 16:11-13 (NLT) teaches us that David was not the first choice of his father Jesse, when Samuel arrived to anoint one of his sons. After having been introduced to seven sons and the oil did not flow, he asked do you have another son. David was the least likely and not even considered by his father. The scripture tells us that God sent Samuel to anoint a new king. That he would anoint the ONE that God names which would be evident when the oil flowed.

David in the fields daily maintaining the sheep was his place of preparation. When you are Positioned to Push you must be Prepared no matter what it is. If God has given you a witty idea, you must research and put the plan in place! Do you know how and where you need to register your business, do you know what school you want to attend to become a nurse, doctor, lawyer, or chef. These are tasks that you will need to accomplish on your own. God will not do these things supernaturally for you. Note... that purpose without a plan is dead from the start.

While David had spent countless hours in the field being seen as meek and too attractive to me one positioned for so great of a position as future king his father did not think he would be chosen but would soon see the oil flow. Listen you are the only one that can stop your purpose from being fulfilled. David had been in a season of preparation learning to protect and lead the sheep; saving them from an attack from a lion being strengthened for him to lead and protect others.

There was a lot of work that went into preparing David for the throne. Not only had he learned to protect, David also had to learn to serve. The current reigning King Saul found himself distressed and called for David to play the harp to calm his spirit which led to him becoming the armor bearer for the King who was sitting in the seat that David would one day possess.

Now David's posture to serve King Saul has POSITIONED him to slay a giant! David's faith in God, allowed him to triumph in war over a giant that was believed to be the fall of the army of King Saul. David convinced King Saul that he had killed a lion and a bear and would surely conquer Goliath the giant. David lived up to the standards that he had set for himself and took a single pebble with a sling shot and slayed the biggest threat to the army.

What is your Goliath, what is stopping you from PUSHING forward? Start the business, write the book, get the degree, masters, and PhD... Push through the travail, every obstacle! To do so, like David was willing to serve King David, position yourself around the right people.

Lastly, as we end this devotion, when a woman is giving birth that is the closest point of death, but they do not stop pushing because if they did there would not be a you nor me! When you are trying to birth something... you must put off your old man, the old nature. The person that you use to be will try to stop you, unmotivating you and making you think that you can not do it, to abort what you are about to delivery.

If you take anything from this devotion you should now be able to put aside self-doubt and take on the bold new man. Be like David a man that walked by faith who overcame obstacles with a single pebble!

David was Positioned, Postured and Prepared!

There is nothing that you can not do, with God all things are possible, so PUSH to your business is formed, until you finish your degree so you an be called Dr!, Judge!, Lawyer!, Chef!, and CEO! Whatever goals you have established and set for yourself as part of your destiny is up to you, PUSH through and do not give up!

CHAPTER 15

Walking in Wisdom

CoAuthor Rev. Tracy Turner

Walking in Wisdom is imperative to the success of life and how to handle people as noted by this devotion's teacher, Rev. Tracy Turner. Rev. Turner advises that you stay aware or beware of those that are trying to connect with you. It is important to understand the value of wisdom and how it should be applied to your everyday life. The teaching for this devotion is focused on Proverbs the book of wisdom which provides good advice for all ages.

Below summarize the benefits in walking in wisdom:

- Chapter one of Proverbs you learn that the fear of the Lord is the beginning of knowledge and wisdom.

- Chapter four indicates that wisdom is the principle thing and the most important thing we can acquire in life.

- Chapter six advises you to avoid making foolish decisions and not be lazy like a sluggard but to be like an ant, industrious.

- Chapter seven provides a warning to stay away from the seductress men and women and avoid adultery by being careful of the company that you keep so that you don't fall into self-destructive traps. There are continuous reminders throughout this chapter that places importance on wisdom and the benefits.

- Chapter eight tells us that wisdom calls out to us and if we are wise, we would answer the call.

- Chapter nine points out the difference between wisdom and foolishness.

- Chapters ten through twenty-four is called "Proverb" and is a series of short saying providing good advice, written by others but collected by Solomon. The saying demonstrates the contrast between being lazy or diligent, foolish, or wicked which admonishes us to have control of our tongue and behavior as well as who you associate with as friends and in business. It gives advice about relationships as well.

- Chapters twenty-five through thirty-one is a collection of writings from Hezekiah with the first section written by Solomon. These writings focus on wisdom for leaders from the least, local, state, and federal government. Proverbs are good for any leader at any compacity or those that aspire to be a leader. I Timothy 2:1-2 (NLT) says, I urge you, first of all, to pray for all people. Ask God to help them; intercede on their behalf and give thanks for them. Pray this way for kings and all who are in authority so that we can live peaceful and quite lives marked by godliness and dignity.

Proverbs thirty–one is noted in the devotion has we compare the Proverbs 31 noble woman to the church because we are the church. The initial versus focus on King Lemuel's respect wise counsel from his mother. The counsel surrounds the character of a good worthy wife. The worthy wife is described as a noble wife as with the church to be honored and respected. We should be like the Jesus Christ and not to bring him harm, having full confidence in him. As the noble wife we too should want to be viewed as worthy, "more than rubies".

The church is not lazy like the Proverbs 31 woman we too are industrious, entrepreneurs willing and able to help the poor. The church should be ready for the winter months, prepared for the winter months clothed with dignity and wisdom. Character and persona are equal to the wife and the church. She speaks wisdom and we as the church should also speak wisdom in all that we do. We should be watchful of affairs and not give way to idols. As the woman doing noble things the church does noble things and will surpass all that was done by them all. While charm is deceiving, a woman who fears the Lord is to be praised! The church that fears the Lord is to be praised!

Before we close, Proverbs 18:22 says that a man that finds a wife/church finds a good thing obtains favor. Ephesians 5:22-23 wives/church must submit to your own church. Revelation 21:9 (NLT) the last book in the bible says, Then one of the seven angels who held the seven bowls containing the seven last plagues came and said to me, "Come with me! I will show you the bride, the wife of the Lamb." This book closes with the infinite knowledge of who we are as the church to God, as the wife/bride of the lamb.